Mel and the Big Mess

Written by Holly Woolnough
Illustrated by Kathryn Inkson

Collins

It is a big mess!

Mel can pack it up.

Pack the lot in sacks.

Toss the socks on top.

It is a big mess!

Mel can fill it up.

Lug bags off the rug.

Tuck the dolls into bed.

It is a big mess!

Mel can pick lots up.

Is it a bad mess?

No, the mess is Tess.

ll

ss

After reading

Letters and Sounds: Phase 2

Word count: 60

Focus phonemes: /g/ /o/ /c/ ck /e/ /u/ /r/ /b/ /f/ ff /l/ ll, ss

Common exception words: the, and, is, into, no

Curriculum links: Personal, social and emotional development

Early learning goals: Reading: read and understand simple sentences; use phonic knowledge to decode regular words and read them aloud accurately; read some common irregular words

Developing fluency

- Your child may enjoy hearing you read the book.
- Take turns to read a page. Encourage your child to read with expression, showing surprise for the sentences ending in an exclamation mark on pages 2, 6 and 10. Check your child notices the question mark on page 12 and reads it appropriately.

Phonic practice

- Take turns to look through pages 2 to 5 to find a word with the /c/ "ck" sound. Together, point to it and sound it out. (page 3 and page 4 p/a/ck – **pack**, page 4 s/a/ck/s – **sacks**, page 5 s/o/ck/s – **socks**)
- Can your child find another "ck" word on page 11? (*pick*)
- Look at the "I spy sounds" pages (14 and 15). Point to the "ll" and "ss" at the top of the pages and ask your child to find things with these spellings in the picture. Prompt by pointing to the doll on page 15 and say: I spy a "ll" in doll. Look for "ll" things first before moving on to "ss" things. (e.g. *ball, bell, windmill, bull, shell, fill (the box); Tess, mess, chess, cross, dress*)

Extending vocabulary

- Ask your child: Can you think of phrases or words that mean the opposite of these?

  big (e.g. *little, small*) **fill it** (*empty it*) **into** (*out of*)
  lots (e.g. *hardly any, not much*) **bad** (e.g. *good, nice*)